Stack Attack

First published by Allen & Unwin in 2017

Allen & Unwin
83 Alexander Street
Crows Nest NSW 2065
Australia
Phone: (61 2) 8425 0100
Email: info@allenandunwin.com
Web: www.allenandunwin.com

A Cataloguing-in-Publication entry is
available from the National Library of Australia
www.trove.nla.gov.au

ISBN 978 1 76029 601 8

For teaching resources, explore
www.allenandunwin.com/resources/for-teachers

Cover and text design by Sandra Nobes
Set in 16 pt ITC Stone Informal by Sandra Nobes
This book was printed in July 2017 at
McPherson's Printing Group, Australia.

1 3 5 7 9 10 8 6 4 2

macparkbooks.com

MIX
Paper from
responsible sources
FSC® C001695
www.fsc.org

The paper in this book is FSC® certified.
FSC® promotes environmentally responsible,
socially beneficial and economically viable
management of the world's forests.

BOOK 5
Stack Attack

MAC PARK

Illustrated by JAMES HART

ALLEN&UNWIN
SYDNEY · MELBOURNE · AUCKLAND · LONDON

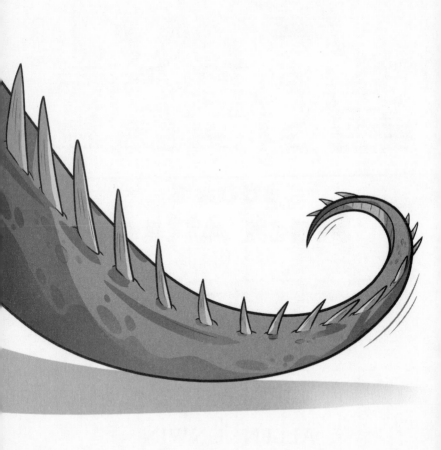

Chapter One

Hunter and Charlie were in the forest, at a waterfall clearing. The biggest dinosaur yet was on the loose. Swinging from its head was another D-Bot Squad member.

The argentinosaurus moved slowly towards Hunter and Charlie. The ground shook with every step it took. Hunter and Charlie's double d-bot rocked from side to side.

Boom! Boom! Boom! Boom!

Hang on tightly, whoever you are, thought Hunter. *It's a long way down from that argentino's neck.*

'I'm glad we've built a high d-bot,' he said to Charlie. 'That argentino is so tall and long. It's bigger than I thought it would be.'

'And wider, too,' Charlie said. 'It's wiping out every tree in its path!'

'I just hope we don't need to fly,' Hunter said. 'Our double d-bot doesn't have wings.'

The argentino's tail swung from side to side, smashing more trees.

Swish! Crunch! Snap! Crash!

'We have to catch this dino – fast!' Charlie cried. 'Soon there won't be any forest left.'

'But we can't teleport the dino yet. We need to save the D-Bot Squad member first,' Hunter said. 'Or else they might fall to the ground when the dino's gone. Or be sent to wherever we send those dinos. We need a plan!'

A flash of light hit the argentino's neck. The dinosaur swung its neck back and lifted its head.

'Roar!'

'Oh no,' Charlie cried. 'The kid's trying to use the teleporting ray on the dino.'

'But it won't work,' Hunter added. 'A dino this big needs two rays at least. They'll just make the argentino grumpy.'

Charlie spoke quickly into her d-band. 'This is Charlie. There are two of us. We're going to help you. Can you hear me?'

A cry came from Hunter and Charlie's d-bands. 'Aaargh!' It was a boy's voice.

'Hey!' Hunter shouted into his d-band. 'Don't use your teleporting ray.'

But there was another flash.
This time, the ray shot right
into the argentino's eye.

The dinosaur rose up on its
back legs. It towered over the
tops of the trees. It was mad.

'**Rooaar!**
Grrrrr!
Rooaar!'

'He can't hear us over the roaring,' Charlie said. 'And now the argentino is super angry.'

Standing on its back legs, the argentino was taller than a ten-floor building. It began to shake its head from side to side.

The D-Bot Squad member bounced around like a tiny rag doll.

'It's trying to shake him off!' cried Hunter. 'He won't be able to hold on much longer. Come on, let's go!'

Chapter Two

Hunter hit the start button on the double d-bot's remote.

'I'll drive,' he said into his helmet mic. 'You use the d-vac to suck up argentino food. We might need it.'

'Hunter,' Charlie said, 'in one day, argentinos ate what we'd eat in two months. More than fifty family-size chocolate cakes. More than 2,000 apples! More than—'

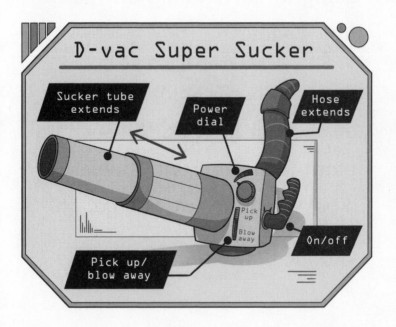

D-vac Super Sucker

Sucker tube
extends

Power
dial

Hose
extends

Pick
up

Blow
away

On/off

Pick up/
blow away

'Charlie,' Hunter said firmly, 'we can do this, okay? Hang on tightly with your legs. We're going to move along this path fast. Ready?'

'Ready,' Charlie said, taking the d-vac from its clips. 'I'll suck up plant food until this double d-bot's belly is full. Go, go, go!'

Hunter drove quickly around
the back of the argentino. Then
he moved along the path the
dino had cleared. There were
plenty of broken plants and
trees for Charlie to suck up.

'I'm fitting a lot in the d-bot's
belly,' she said.

Press and pack

Hunter spun the double d-bot around and hurried back to the argentino. 'I'll slow the d-bot down now,' he said. 'Try reaching the boy with your d-vac.'

Just then, a voice boomed through their d-band speakers. 'I can't teleport this dino alone. Use your rays too, so we can send it home. Hurry!'

The dino had stopped roaring. Charlie spoke into her d-band.

'This is Charlie. We can't use the rays yet. Once that dinosaur is gone, you'll fall to the ground. **Or you might go with it!** We have to get you down. We have a plan, but you'll need to trust us. What's your name?'

'Ethan,' the voice replied. 'I'd just caught a baby allosaurus when this one turned up. I thought I could get it too. But it got me instead.'

Hunter smiled. 'The same thing happened to me, Ethan. We're going to move in to the argentino's leg now. Just do what Charlie says. I'm Hunter.'

'This d-vac is super-strong,' Charlie told Ethan. 'And it has extra-long poles inside. When we get close, I'll point it at your back. You'll get sucked onto the d-vac, okay? Then I'll bring you down to our double d-bot. Let go when I say so.'

'Got it,' Ethan replied.

'Hunter, watch out!' Charlie cried suddenly.

But it was too late. The argentino had whipped its tail. It hit the double d-bot, sending it into a tail spin.

Hunter dropped the speed and held on tightly. When the d-bot stopped spinning, he called out to Charlie. 'Okay up there?'

'That was way better than dodgem cars,' she replied. 'But let's watch out for tails this time.'

'Yep, going in again,' Hunter said.

This time, he moved the double d-bot more slowly. When Hunter reached the argentino's back leg, he hit the stop button.

You're almost as tall as a giraffe, thought Hunter. *You're so awesome!*

'Now!' Charlie shouted. Hunter looked up and saw Ethan sucked onto the d-vac.

'See you soon,' Hunter whispered to the argentino. 'When we have a teleporting plan we know will work!'

Chapter Three

They sped away into the forest.
Charlie pointed the d-vac – and
Ethan – downwards.

'Grab the extend-o-rods and
slide down to Hunter,' she said.
'I'm turning the d-vac off now.'

'Good job,' Hunter said when Ethan was sitting safely behind him. 'I'm Hunter, and you know Charlie. So, where's your d-bot?'

Ethan pointed to a clump of trees ahead. 'Behind those trees. It's a mess, though. I'll have to build a new one back at base.'

But Hunter wasn't so sure.
'Let's take a look. There might
be parts we could use.'

They pulled up at what was left
of Ethan's d-bot.

Charlie gasped. 'It's smashed to
bits! I'm so glad you weren't
hurt. You were very lucky.'

Ethan climbed off the double
d-bot and looked at the wreck.

'The argentino picked my d-bot
up in its mouth. It bit down on
it. That was when I grabbed
onto the dino's neck. I made
my d-bot green, so I could hide
easily in the trees. Dumb idea.
Very dumb idea!'

Charlie joined Ethan on the ground. 'The dino thought your d-bot was a plant?' she asked.

'Yes,' Ethan said, 'and spat my d-bot out fast. It hit the ground and broke into pieces. Then the argentino walked right over it.'

Hunter looked through the mess. 'Some bits are still okay, though.'

Boom! Rumble! Thump! Boom!

The ground beneath the D-Bot
Squad members shook. The
double d-bot rocked from side
to side.

'It feels like an earthquake!'
Ethan said.

'Hold the double d-bot steady,'
Charlie said, climbing on. 'I'm
going up to take a look.'

Rumble! Slap! Boom! Rumble!

Charlie sat on top of the double d-bot. She hit her remote's full-circle button. Slowly, the top part of her d-bot turned. When she was facing the other way, she hit stop.

Ethan grinned. 'You two sure know how to build d-bots.'

'Sometimes,' Hunter said, smiling.

Charlie looked out over the treetops. 'It's moved. And you won't believe this – there's another argentino! It looks like they're fighting. We have to stop them.'

Thoughts filled Hunter's head.

'Maybe we don't need to be big after all,' Hunter said. 'Those argentinos are slow, but their tails are not.'

Charlie climbed back down. 'So we need to be small and fast!' she said.

'Oh! What about building three small, fast d-bots?' Ethan asked. 'Could we do that?'

'We'll have to,' Hunter answered.
'It will take three rays per dino
to send these two back.'

Charlie looked the double d-bot
up and down. Then she stared
at what was left of Ethan's
d-bot. She was deep in thought.
Hunter waited quietly, knowing
now how her mind worked.

'The velociraptor is known as the
speedy thief,' Charlie said finally.

'That's exactly what we need
to build, then!' Hunter cried.
'Bird-like raptors! Super-fast.
Turkey-sized. But ours will fly!'

Charlie looked at Ethan. 'Yours won't fly, though,' she said gently. 'My old single d-bot's wings can make two new small sets. But your d-bot's wings are totally trashed.'

'Two flying bots and one ground bot will work,' said Hunter.

'It's perfect for teleporting two massive argentinos locked in battle!' Charlie added.

'Wait! How will our dino-food fit into a tiny belly?' asked Hunter.

'I've got a flat-pack-backpack,' Ethan said. 'It shrinks things down to a tiny size!'

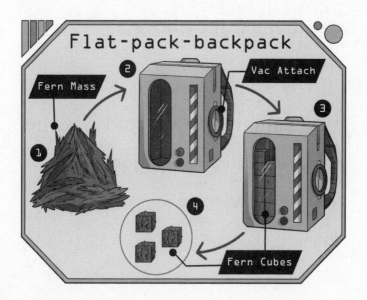

Flat-pack-backpack

Fern Mass

2

Vac Attach

3

1

4

Fern Cubes

'Cool!' said Charlie. 'That's exactly what we need.'

'Okay,' said Hunter. 'I'll fly around the dinos' heads and ray them from above.'

'I'll ray from above as well, but target their bellies,' said Charlie. 'Their middles are bigger than two whales!'

'And I'll come up behind them,'
Ethan said. 'Between us, we'll
have these two dinos covered.
It's a good plan. Let's get to
work.'

Chapter Four

Three newly built d-bots now stood where Ethan's old one had lain smashed. The squad members looked them over one last time. They were happy with their work.

'I'm glad we used the extend-o-rods for your tail, Ethan,' Charlie said.

Ethan hit the tail button on his new remote. He watched as the tail became long, then short again. 'It's so quick!' he said, smiling.

'You'll need it on the ground,' Hunter said. 'Those argentino tails are very powerful.'

'Well, I think we're ready,'
Charlie said.

Rumble! **Slap! Boom! Rumble!**

'Who knows how many trees
they've smashed already,' Ethan
said. 'We'd better go find them.'

'Helmets on! Remotes clipped to
belts!' Hunter said. 'These
d-bots are going to move as
fast as racing cars.'

'Let's find those suckers,' Charlie said.

Rumble! Boom! Roar!

Hunter nodded. *'Go!'*

The d-bots took off at top speed. Charlie and Hunter zipped in and out of trees and branches. Ethan's d-bot ran so fast it looked like a blur.

Whoosh!

They found the dinos at the waterfall. The three squad members hid among some trees, wide-eyed.

'They've cleared heaps and heaps of trees!' Charlie gasped. 'We haven't been gone very long. What a mess.'

'They'll eat our hiding spot next,' Ethan said. 'It's the only clump of trees left standing!'

'They break apart to eat, and then come back together again,' Hunter said. 'I think they're playing with each other. Not fighting.'

Boom! Rumble! Boom! Crash! Rumble! Swish!

Ethan's d-bot almost fell over.

'Woah,' Ethan cried. 'That's like two big jumbo jets hitting the ground! Up close, it will be hard to keep my d-bot on its legs. I wish I was a bit bigger right now. These d-bots are so shrimpy!'

'We can do it, Ethan,' said Hunter.

'Okay, I'll fly to the left,' said Charlie. 'Hunter, you fly to the right. Ethan, you stay hidden until we're ready in the air. We all go in together, okay?'

'Okay!' said Hunter and Ethan at the same time.

Flrrrrrppppppttttt! Phrrrrrrrrrrr!

Flrrrrrpppppptttttt!
Braaaaapt!

'Uh-oh!' Charlie groaned as she flew off to the left. 'Toxic farts again. Masks on, everyone.'

Hunter and Ethan hit the mask button on their helmets. 'Good luck!' Hunter said to Ethan. Then he flew off to the right.

Hunter's idea worked. The argentinos munched on Charlie's food-drop. Their heads were close together as they ate. While they were busy, Charlie sucked up all the poo with the d-vac.

Ethan was free, but he was not happy. He wiped dino-poo from his helmet's visor. Then he said, 'Let's get those two!'

'Oh, we've made a mistake,' Hunter cried. 'The rule is to teleport from *above*!'

Charlie groaned. 'Of course,' she said. 'Ethan, climb onto my back. We'll ray their bellies and legs. Quick! The food is running out.'

The three D-Bot Squad members moved into place. **'Three, two, one...now!'** Hunter called.

Ethan's teleporting ray shot out
over the argentinos' back legs.
Charlie's hit their bellies.
Hunter's ray covered their heads.
Instantly, they began to vanish.

Chapter Five

Later, Charlie and Hunter sat by the waterfall.

'Those dinos were the hardest yet,' Charlie said. 'Do you think there could be more of them?'

Hunter shrugged. 'I wondered the same thing. Although we didn't see any others when we were flying around.'

Ethan stepped out from under the waterfall. He shook his head. Water flew from his curls onto Charlie and Hunter.

'Hey,' Hunter said, laughing. 'Are you sure you're totally clean?'

'Do I still smell?' Ethan asked.

'No,' Charlie said. 'And luckily for you, these suits are quick-dry! Dino Corp has thought of everything.'

'Do you ever wonder about the Dino Corp safe place? The place we send these dinosaurs back to?' Hunter asked. 'And how many dinosaurs have got out?'

Before anyone could answer,
all three d-bands flashed. Ms
Stegg's voice boomed from their
speakers. 'You caught them
both. Top work, all of you. Now
you must come back to base.'

'Are there more argentinos on
the loose?' Charlie asked.

'No,' replied Ms Stegg. 'It's
something else. Teleport to base,
please. Over and out.'

'That doesn't sound good,'
Charlie said, standing up. 'We'd
better get going.'

'She sure sounded rushed,'
Ethan added.

Hunter bit his lip. 'I wonder what we're in for next?'

'I guess we're about to find out,' said Charlie.

The D-Bot Squad members climbed onto their d-bots. On the count of three, they pushed their teleport buttons. And before they knew it, they were back at base.

'Welcome back,' said Ms Stegg.

She handed them a bowl of pasta and a banana smoothie each.

'We've found a kronosaurus in the sea. Maybe more than one. You'll need to go as a team. Work together to build your new d-bots. You can eat your lunch as you work.'

But Hunter barely looked at the food. He was busy thinking.

Kronosaurus
(cron-oh-saw-rus)

● The giant of the sea.
● Not a dinosaur – a pliosaur!
● Jaws stronger than a T-rex's.

The Kron!

meat-eaters!

We don't want to be their lunch!

'Krons ate anything and everything in the sea,' Charlie said. 'The sea life around them will be eaten in no time.'

'Correct,' Ms Stegg said, handing them each water jet packs and new helmets. 'But you'll find a way to stop them. Now, I'm sorry, but I need to check some other alerts.'

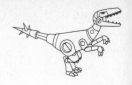

Ethan chewed on his pasta. 'We'll need to both swim and fly,' he mumbled. 'But how can we stop them eating **everything** in the sea?'

'I'm not sure yet. Maybe we can catch them with super-strong nets, though,' Charlie said. 'Then teleport them.'

'And we'll need deep-sea lights,' Hunter added.

'Have we missed anything?' Ethan asked, staring at the screen.

'That massive moss worked so well with the steg,' Charlie said. 'We might need that trick again. Let's take some spray that smells like yummy kron food.'

'Good thinking!' Hunter said. 'We're all sorted now.'

They hit the screen's parts
button. Parts flew out of a
chute on the far wall.

Whoosh! Clang! Whoosh!

'Let's get building,' Hunter said.
'Sea life is being eaten every
minute!'

Soon, the d-bots were ready.
The team put on their new
helmets and water jet packs.

'We go together, team,' Hunter
said firmly.

The three squad members
climbed onto their new d-bots.

'This is my first underwater
mission,' Charlie said.

'Mine too,' Ethan said. 'Are we
good to go?'

'Yes,' said Charlie and Hunter.

They hit their teleporting
buttons on the count of three.

And then they were gone.

The team found themselves close to the ocean floor. It was eerily quiet. The ocean was so dark they couldn't see anything.

Ethan hit the spotlight on his d-bot. It lit up a wide circle of water in front of them.

And staring straight at them were five krons...their mouths open wide.

How will D-Bot Squad
get out of this one?
Read Book 6, *Deep Dive*,
to find out...